Investigating Desire

A Grumpy Detective Sworn Off Love, a Fearless Journalist, and a Slow-Burn, High-Stakes Romance

Hana York

Pink Pop Publishing

Investigating Desire

(Hearts on Duty Book 4)

Copyright © 2025 by Hana York

www.HanaYork.com

Contents

Chapter One

♥

NATE

D awn broke over the crime scene, the early light catching the jagged edges of broken glass scattered across the sidewalk. I stood still, letting the weight of another robbery press against the already tense muscles in my shoulders. Through the smashed storefront window, I spotted an overturned cash register, receipts, and loose bills littering the floor like discarded confetti. A mess. Like every other damn break-in this month.

I yanked out my notepad, scribbling the exact same details I'd written five times before. New location, identical story: no sign of forced entry, zero leads worth following. Another case destined for the unsolved pile.

"Detective Whitaker?"

The sharp, self-assured voice sliced through the background noise of radio static and cop chatter. I exhaled slowly, bracing myself for yet another store owner demanding answers I didn't have. But when I turned, I was met with something else entirely.

She stood just beyond the yellow tape, all poise and sharp angles—long black hair falling well past her shoulders, piercing silver-blue eyes locking onto mine with a mix of determination and something that looked suspiciously like amusement. In her hand, a notepad and pen, held like a weapon.

"Tessa Donovan," she said, stepping forward like she belonged here. "I'm the journalist assigned to shadow you for the piece on law enforcement and the recent robberies."

Shadow me? My grip on the notepad tightened as I let my gaze flick from her face to the press badge clipped to her coat.

I didn't take the hand she extended. "Shadow me?" I said flatly, making no effort to hide my irritation.

"That's right." Her voice was smooth, unbothered by my less-than-welcoming tone. "I'm here to capture the human side of the investigation. The public loves to see the story behind the badge."

I snorted, shaking my head as I went back to my notes. "Great. That's exactly what we need—more people in the middle of a crime scene."

"I don't need your permission to do my job," she shot back, unfazed. "Just access. Which, by the way, your captain already approved."

I stopped writing mid-sentence, my jaw ticking. "Of course he did," I muttered under my breath.

I glanced back at her. She watched me closely, the corners of her lips tilted slightly like she knew I was two seconds from telling her to take her notepad and shove it.

"Ms. Donovan, this isn't some publicity stunt," I said flatly

"You think I don't know that?" She moved closer, glass crackling under her boots. "I'm not here for a photo op. I want the real story—the one that happens when the cameras leave, and people like you get to work."

A flicker of something twisted in my chest—annoyance, mostly. But also something close to grudging respect. She didn't scare easily; I'd give her that.

I met her gaze, letting the silence stretch between us. "Fine," I said finally. "Observe all you want. But don't get in my way, and don't expect me to slow down to explain things."

She smiled, flipping open her notepad like she'd already won. "Wouldn't dream of it," she murmured, pen moving fast across the page.

I sighed, already regretting every single life choice that led to this moment.

This was going to be a long damn assignment.

***

Tessa dusted a few flecks of dust from her jeans, utterly unfazed by the chaos around her. "So, Detective," she said, her voice smooth, confident. "What's your read on this?"

I hesitated, watching her. Most reporters would have come in with their own half-baked theories, fishing for a quote to spin whatever angle they wanted. But her eyes held something different—genuine curiosity. Against my better judgment, I answered.

"Could pass for a smash and grab," I muttered, waving a hand at the mess. "Looks random, but something about it doesn't sit quite right."

She jotted something down, nodding. "Connected to the other break-ins?"

"Can't say yet," I said, stepping toward the register.

As I moved, I caught the faintest trace of her perfume—something savory. I ignored how it tugged at the edges of my awareness, forcing my focus back on the scene.

"What's your take?" The words left my mouth before I could stop them.

Tessa blinked, clearly surprised. "You're actually asking me?"

I shrugged. "You're here. Might as well see if you've got anything useful to add."

Her pen drummed against the notepad as she sized me up, considering the invitation. After a moment's deliberation, she moved beside me with that same confident precision, taking care not to disturb anything at the scene.

"Well, since you're curious..." She crouched slightly, tracing the air above the debris. "See how the glass sprayed outward? That means they broke it from the inside."

My eyebrows lifted slightly. "Pretty sharp for a reporter."

Tessa shot me a half smile that said she knew exactly how good she was at her job. "Been around enough crime scenes," she said lightly, but I didn't miss the note of satisfaction in her voice.

Our eyes met, and the space between us shifted.

I knew that feeling. That unwanted pull, the one that crept up when you least expected it, the one I'd buried under long work hours and a firm no-relationships policy.

I cleared my throat and looked away first, dragging my attention back to the register.

This was a distraction I didn't need. I had a caseload stacked a mile high, a city full of criminals who didn't seem to take a damn night off, and a personal life I'd long since given up trying to fix.

The last thing I needed was some smart-mouthed journalist getting under my skin.

And yet, as I scanned the ransacked shop, my gaze kept finding her. The way she bit her lower lip in concentration as she scribbled notes. How the early morning light caught subtle hints of silver in her dark hair. The way she tilted her head, completely focused, like she was trying to see past the obvious.

I exhaled sharply, forcing myself to look anywhere else.

Nope. Not happening.

I'd sworn off love for a reason. And no amount of sharp wit and striking blue eyes would make me forget that.

Get it together, Whitaker.

Damnit, I was so screwed.

I exhaled sharply, snapping my notepad shut. "We're done here," I announced, voice gruff. "I need to head back to the station and start processing."

Tessa tucked her pen behind her ear and slipped her notepad into her bag. "Same. My editor's expecting an update."

We stepped out into the late morning heat, the humidity thick enough to choke on. I loosened the collar of my shirt, rolling my shoulders as sweat gathered at the base of my neck. Tessa, on the other hand, looked impossibly cool, the sun catching in her long, dark hair.

I shouldn't have been looking. But I was.

"I'll—" I cleared my throat, ignoring the way my voice had gone rough. "I'll check in later. See if you need clarification on anything."

Tessa arched an eyebrow. "Clarification?" she echoed, lips twitching. "Is that your way of saying you're looking forward to talking to me, Detective?"

I scowled, patting my pockets for my keys just to give my hands something to do. "It's my way of saying I don't want you getting the facts wrong."

"Mm," she hummed, clearly not buying it.

I finally found my keys and latched onto the distraction. "Well. Duty calls."

Tessa leaned lazily against the doorframe, crossing her arms. "Until next time, Detective," she murmured, voice laced with something dark and sexy.

I nearly dropped my keys.

I was so screwed.

I climbed into my car and cranked the AC to full blast, letting the icy air hit my overheated skin. My grip tightened on the steering wheel, knuckles turning white as I forced a steady breath through my nose.

What the hell was wrong with me?

I was a professional, not some lovesick idiot getting tripped up by sharp blue eyes and a knowing smile. But as I pulled away from the curb, my gaze betrayed me, flicking to the rearview mirror.

Tessa stood on the sidewalk, arms crossed, watching me go.

For a split second, our eyes met in the reflection. A jolt shot through me—sharp, undeniable.

"Stop it," I muttered under my breath, jaw clenching. I smacked my palm against the steering wheel for good measure. "Not interested. Not happening."

I ran through the logical, *practical* reasons why this was a bad idea. She was a journalist, and I was a detective. Two opposing forces, fundamentally at odds. And even if I ignored that, I had no business looking at anyone like that, not after everything. I was still picking up the damn pieces from my divorce, still figuring out who I was now that marriage wasn't part of the equation. The last thing I needed was a complication like Tessa Donovan.

Besides, she was probably just being friendly. Professional. This was nothing more than an overactive imagination fueled by too many months of keeping my head down and my life as simple as possible.

I refocused on the road, trying to force out the image of the curve of her lips when she pushed my buttons just to see if I'd push back.

Work. That's where I needed to keep my focus.

Not on Tessa.

Definitely not on her.

TESSA

I stood on the sidewalk, arms crossed, watching Nate's car disappear down the street. I let out a slow breath, willing my pulse to settle, but my body still hummed with the tension that had crackled between us.

Damn him.

I turned toward my car, but my mind wasn't anywhere near the present. It was stuck on sharp green eyes that saw too much, the firm set of his jaw, the way his broad shoulders filled out his shirt just right.

I swallowed hard, biting my lip as a dangerous thought crept in—what would those shoulders look like without the shirt?

Heat crawled up my neck, and I shook my head, cursing under my breath as I yanked the door open. This was ridiculous. I was here for a story, not to get sidetracked by some grumpy, frustratingly attractive detective.

And yet, I couldn't stop thinking about him.

Sliding into the driver's seat, I blasted the AC, hoping it would cool me down. It didn't. Instead, the memory of his voice—low and rough when he leaned in close to point out evidence—played on repeat in my head. His fingers had brushed against mine, and his hands felt rough, calloused, and capable.

I gripped the steering wheel tighter. *What would those hands feel like on my skin?*

I exhaled sharply, shaking my head as if I could physically shake off the thought. *Get it together, Tessa.*

The drive back to the office didn't help. I wasn't looking for complications—hadn't been for a long time. I had a career to focus on, a life I'd built on my own.

But Nate Whitaker?

He was the kind of man who could make me forget every reason I'd sworn off distractions.

Hours later, my phone buzzed against the wood. I grabbed it, my breath catching at the unknown number lighting up the screen.

"Something big going down at the marina tonight—slip 11. You didn't hear it from me."

Adrenaline spiked in my veins.

This could be it. The break I'd been chasing.

I hesitated, fingers hovering over my phone. I should call Nate and let him know about the tip. But then again, I didn't work for him. I had a story to chase, and some handsome detective with a bad attitude wasn't going to steal my thunder. Not this time.

To hell with it.

I snatched my bag and keys.

This one was mine.

Chapter Two

♥

NATE

The marina stretched before me, shrouded in the dusky glow of fading daylight. The scent of salt and fish clung to the humid air, mixing with the distant hum of boat engines further down the pier. I cut the engine and sat for a beat, scanning the docks. Too quiet. At this hour, there should've been at least a few stragglers—fishermen wrapping up for the night, deckhands securing lines—but the slips were nearly deserted.

Unease curled in my gut.

Stepping out, my boots crunched against the gravel, the sound unnaturally loud in the silence. The marina's floodlights cast long, warped shadows across the water, making every shape distorted and unfamiliar. I loosened my shoulders, keeping one hand near my holstered weapon as I made my way down the dock.

Slip 11.

The yacht docked there stood out like a sore thumb—pristine white against the weathered vessels surrounding it, polished where the others were rust-streaked and worn. The name *Siren's Call* gleamed in gold lettering on the stern, but something about it scratched at the back of my mind, a memory just out of reach.

I climbed onto the deck, the wood creaking softly under my weight. Everything about the boat felt... off. Too still. Too clean. The faint scent of perfume clung to the air, mysteriously familiar and an odd contrast to the brine and diesel of the marina.

Hand near my weapon, I moved toward the cabin, every muscle coiled tight. The door wasn't locked. That alone set off warning bells. I gripped the handle, easing it open with controlled precision.

And then—movement.

I caught the flicker of a shadow near a built-in desk, the soft rustle of paper shifting. My heart slammed once, twice—before my brain caught up to my eyes.

Tessa.

She froze mid-motion, fingers curled tight around a handful of documents, her sharp blue eyes locking onto mine.

I exhaled sharply, moving my hand away from my gun, but my voice came out rough. "Tessa?"

She clutched the papers against her chest, shoulders squared. "Well, this is awkward," she said, her voice only slightly uneven.

I dragged a hand through my hair, biting back a curse. "What the hell are you doing here? This is an active investigation," I said, stepping inside and closing the door behind me. "You need to leave."

Tessa lifted her chin, every inch of her radiating defiance. "Got a tip something big was going down tonight," she said. "Figured I'd check it out."

My jaw clenched. *Of course she did.*

"You have any idea how dangerous this is?" I took another step closer, my body vibrating with frustration. "These aren't your run-of-the-mill burglars. You can't just waltz into the middle of—"

"I can handle myself."

Like hell she could.

I crossed the cabin quickly, closing the space between us before she could toss out another reckless excuse.

"You don't even know what you just walked into," I ground out.

Tessa's breath hitched, but she didn't back down. If anything, her grip on those stolen papers tightened, her silver-blue eyes flashing with something just as sharp as my own frustration.

I stepped closer, closing the remaining space between us. Tessa held her ground, but I caught the flicker of awareness in her sharp blue eyes, the subtle hitch in her breath as she registered just how little room was left between us.

Her back met the edge of the desk. Nowhere to go. Nowhere to run.

"You're in way over your head," I murmured.

Tessa's pulse jumped in her throat, but she held my gaze, her expression unreadable. "I'm just doing my job," she said, her voice quieter now. Steadier than I expected.

My jaw tightened. *That* was the problem.

"Your job isn't worth your life." The words came out like gravel, frustration simmering beneath them.

Tessa opened her mouth, maybe to argue, maybe to tell me exactly where I could shove my concern—but voices drifted in from the dock before she could.

I stiffened, instincts firing to high alert.

"Shit," I muttered, already moving.

In one swift motion, I grabbed her arm and yanked her into the narrow closet tucked against the cabin's far wall. The door shut behind us just as heavy footsteps hit the deck above.

The closet was damn near suffocating—small, dark, cramped, with shelves behind me and Tessa pressed tight against my chest.

Her breath came in shallow, quick bursts, matching my own. My hands held her waist, holding her still as we listened, frozen.

I felt her tense against me, her body molding against mine in a way that should not have sent heat curling through my gut.

But it did.

I exhaled slowly, fighting against every ounce of awareness flooding my system.

Because the real danger?

It wasn't just outside that door.

TESSA

The deck groaned above, heavy boots moving across the planks with slow, deliberate purpose. My pulse thundered, pounding against my ribs as Nate's arms tightened around me, holding me still. His breath was warm against my ear, sending a shiver down my spine despite the real danger surrounding us.

"Search below," a gruff voice ordered. "Every corner."

I went completely still, barely daring to breathe.

Nate's grip tightened around my waist, his mouth brushing the shell of my ear. "Don't make a sound," he murmured, his voice so low I barely caught it.

I nodded once, fighting to steady my breathing.

A door creaked. Someone entered the cabin.

My entire body went rigid as I pressed myself instinctively back against Nate. His arms flexed around me, solid, reassuring. Protective.

The light passed over the closet door. The footsteps halted outside the closet door.

We both froze.

The space was too small, too warm, and every point of contact between us was a fresh kind of torture. Nate's body was hard muscle, every inch of him pressing against me in a way I knew I shouldn't be noticing. But I did. I noticed everything.

His chest rose and fell in a measured rhythm against my back. His scent—clean, woodsy, something undeniably male—wrapped around me, making it impossible to focus on anything but *him*.

I shifted ever so slightly. A mistake.

Because the second I moved, I became painfully aware of the unmistakable hardness pressed against my backside.

A slow, simmering heat curled in my belly.

Nate's breath hitched. His hands tensed at my waist.

I knew I should ignore it. That now, of all times, wasn't the moment to dwell on the fact that his body was reacting to mine. But my traitorous brain didn't care.

My pulse pounded so loudly that I was sure whoever was outside the closet could hear it. Every nerve in my body was hyperaware of Nate—of the way his jaw clenched near my temple, the way his fingers curled slightly into my hips like he was barely holding himself in check.

The moment stretched unbearably long.

Then, finally, the boots outside the closet started moving again.

"All clear down here," someone called.

Nate's grip on me loosened slightly, but he didn't let go. Outside, muffled voices carried from the deck above, the clink of bottles and low murmurs signaling that whoever had boarded the boat wasn't leaving anytime soon.

"They're settling in for the long haul," Nate whispered against my ear.

A shiver chased down my spine, though I wasn't sure if it was from his words or how his breath sent warmth skimming across my neck.

"What do we do now?" I whispered, my voice barely more than a breath.

Nate's fingers flexed at my hips; his body still impossibly close. "We wait," he murmured, his voice rougher than before.

Waiting sounded logical. Smart. Safe.

But in the tight, stifling darkness of the closet, with Nate pressed so firmly against me, waiting felt like the hardest damn thing I'd ever have to do.

I shifted, trying to relieve the burning ache in my core, but only succeeded in pressing back against Nate's arousal. His sharp intake of breath cut through the darkness.

"Tessa," he warned, his voice low and rough.

I turned my head, our faces now inches apart in the darkness. "What?" I whispered innocently, though there was nothing innocent about the way I deliberately rolled my hips back against him, feeling his hardness press more firmly against me. A soft groan escaped his lips before he could stop it.

"We can't," he whispered hoarsely, even as his hands tightened on my waist. "It's too dangerous."

But I was beyond caring about danger. The heat between us had ignited into an inferno, overwhelming my senses.

"I don't care," I breathed, my lips a hairsbreadth from his. "I want you, Nate."

Nate's control snapped. Tightening his hold on my hips he pulled me roughly back against his body so that his hard cock was pressed firmly against my backside.

"Fuck, Tessa," he growled in my ear as he ground against my ass.

Nate's fingers found the hem of my blouse, slipping underneath to caress the soft skin of my stomach. I gasped as his hand moved higher, cupping my breast through the silk of my bra. His thumb brushed over my hardened nipple, sending sparks of pleasure through my body.

"Nate," I breathed as he pinched my nipple. His lips moved to my neck, nipping and sucking. I rocked back against him, needing more. Nate's free hand trailed down my stomach, deftly unfastening my pants.

I whimpered softly, pressing closer.

"Shh," Nate murmured against her lips. "We have to be quiet."

He slipped his fingers inside my pants, stroking my pussy through my underwear.

My head fell back against Nate's chest as he slipped his fingers beneath the silk of my underwear. I was wet and ready for him and had to bite my lip to keep from begging him to fuck me.

"God, you're so wet," Nate groaned softly, his voice rough with need.

Nate's fingers slid through my slick folds, teasing and exploring. I bit back a moan as he circled my clit with agonizing slowness. His other hand continued kneading my breast, pinching and rolling my nipple between his fingers.

"Is this what you want?" he demanded, his voice a low rumble against my ear.

I nodded frantically, beyond words, as Nate slipped two thick fingers inside me. My inner walls clenched around him, drawing him deeper. He pumped his fingers in a steady rhythm, curling them to hit that perfect spot with each thrust.

My hips rocked against his hand, chasing more friction. Nate's thumb found my clit again, rubbing tight circles as his fingers worked me from the inside. Pleasure built rapidly, coiling tighter and tighter in my core.

Nate's breathing became ragged in my ear, his chest heaving against my back as his fingers relentlessly stroked me closer and closer to the edge. His erection pressed into my backside, a testament to his own arousal.

I arched my back grinding against him. "Don't stop." I panted out, squeezing my eyes shut as the coil of pleasure inside me tightened.

Determined to feel every sensation, I rocked back and forth, taking him deeper. Nate growled low in his throat and obliged me, picking up the pace. His thumb flicked over my swollen clit in time with his thrusts, sending an exquisite wave of pleasure through me. My body trembled, every nerve alive with sensation as I balanced on the razor's edge of climax.

"Come for me," Nate whispered, his voice rough and commanding.

His words sent me spiraling over the edge. My inner walls clenched around his fingers as waves of intense pleasure crashed over me. I bit my lip hard to stifle my cries, my body shaking as Nate worked me through my orgasm.

As the aftershocks faded, I sagged back against Nate's solid chest, breathing heavily. He slowly withdrew his fingers, and I had to bite back a whimper at the loss.

We stood perfectly still in the darkness for a long moment, our ragged breathing the only sound. Reality slowly crept back in—the cramped closet, the danger lurking just outside.

Chapter Three

❤

NATE

As the haze of pleasure burned away, reality came crashing in like a cold wave. My eyes snapped open, my pulse still hammering, but not from desire anymore. Silence. The voices and footsteps above had disappeared.

Shit.

I pulled away from Tessa, barely resisting the urge to punch the closet door. We missed everything.

"They're gone," I muttered, shoving the door open with enough force to rattle the frame. I stalked into the now-empty cabin, my entire body rigid with frustration.

Tessa followed, her hands smoothing over her clothes, cheeks flushed. "Nate, please—"

"Don't," I cut in, my voice sharp, cold. I raked a hand through my hair, scanning the abandoned space. "We missed it. We could have heard everything. They could've been laying out their entire operation; instead, we were too—" I gritted my teeth, biting off the rest of that thought before making it worse.

Tessa flinched but lifted her chin. "I'm sorry," she said, quieter this time. "I didn't mean—"

"You had no right interfering with my investigation," I hissed, turning on her. My voice was low, controlled—but barely. "Not only did you blow months of work, but you nearly got us both caught."

I started pacing, trying to rein in the fury coursing through me. Every muscle in my body was taut, adrenaline still surging, mixing with something darker.

The memory of Tessa's body pressed against mine in that cramped closet momentarily flooded my senses. Her soft curves molding to my hard planes, the intoxicating scent of her perfume mixed with arousal, the breathy little gasps she made as I touched her.

I squeezed his eyes shut for a second, willing away the vivid images, but it was useless. My body still thrummed with unfulfilled need, my cock still partially hard. Christ, I'd been so close to losing it completely, rutting against her like some horny teenager. The friction from her backside grinding against me had nearly pushed me over the edge.

I needed space, needed to get my head on straight before I did something even more reckless.

"Look," I said, my voice low, measured. "This thing between us—whatever the hell it is—won't work."

Tessa's lips parted, her sharp intake of breath slicing through the silence, but I held up a hand before she could argue.

"You're a distraction I can't afford right now," I bit out, forcing steel into my voice, even as the words felt like swallowing glass.

Her eyes flashed, quick and sharp. "A distraction?" she repeated like she couldn't believe I'd actually said it. "Need I remind you, Detective Whitaker—" my name rolled off her tongue like a curse, "that I'm not here by accident? This isn't some pet project I picked up for fun. My editor put me on this case. My career depends on it."

She stepped closer, her voice dropping, turning razor-sharp. "I know things between us are messy, but you don't get to push me off this story just because you've got regrets. I've got deadlines to meet, and you've got a job to do."

I clenched my fists, fighting the urge to look away. Damn it, she was right.

Captain Reeves had made that clear enough, "*Cooperate with the press, Whitaker, for once in your damn life.*"

That didn't mean I had to like it.

"Fine," I muttered, the word barely scraping past my teeth. "You're here on assignment. But that doesn't change the fact that what just happened was a mistake. One that won't happen again."

For half a second, something flickered in her expression. Something I didn't want to name. But just as fast, she shut it down.

"Agreed," she said coolly. "We're professionals. We put this behind us and focus on the case."

I nodded curtly, ignoring how my body thrummed with residual heat. Ignoring the way her cheeks were still flushed from desire.

I forced myself to look away. "We should get out of here before someone comes back."

We slipped off the yacht without another word, moving silently down the gangplank. The humid night air clung to my skin, doing nothing to cool the fire still burning in my veins. The water lapped lazily at the dock, the marina eerily quiet.

Tessa walked beside me, clutching her notepad against her chest, her usual confidence a little shaken. Good. She damn well should be.

The gravel crunched under our feet as we reached the parking lot. My gut twisted as I turned to her. "Head straight home," I muttered, my voice harsher than intended.

She hesitated, glancing up at me in the dim light. Her brows furrowed like she was about to argue, but then something softened. She must have caught the tension in my jaw, the fact that, for all my gruffness, I was worried.

"I can handle myself, Detective," she said, quieter this time. Then, after a beat, "But... thanks."

TESSA

Instead of going home, I headed into the office. My pulse was still thrumming, my skin still overheated from our encounter in the closet—from him. But it wasn't just the heat lingering in my veins. It was the audacity of Nate Whitaker brushing me off like I was some rookie playing journalist.

Like I wasn't damn good at what I did.

I gripped the steering wheel tighter, trying to focus on the road instead of the memory of his body pressed against mine, the feel of his rough hands, the way his breath had gone ragged when I shifted against him. The way he had made me come. A shiver ran down my spine, and I cursed under my breath.

I had bigger things to worry about than how good Nate made me feel.

At my desk, I leaned toward my laptop screen, fine-tuning the final words of my article. The pattern in the robberies wasn't random—it led straight to one of Anchor Bay's untouchables, the connection to Rick Hayes was impossible to ignore. My cursor hovered over the publish button for half a second before I clicked.

This story would kick the hornet's nest, but that was the job. The truth wouldn't expose itself.

I was almost midnight by the time I left the newsroom and the parking lot was bathed in deep shadows. I walked toward my car, mentally running through my to-do list for tomorrow, when I spotted an note tucked under my windshield wiper.

I stopped cold.

My name was scrawled across the front in jagged, hurried letters.

The uneasy prickle at the back of my neck intensified as I reached for it, my fingers trembling slightly as I unfolded the note. The words slashed through my earlier sense of triumph, each letter a cold blade against my skin.

Stay out of things that don't concern you, or you'll regret it.

The air in my lungs turned to stone.

I snapped my head up, scanning the lot. Every shadow felt threatening, and every parked car was a potential hiding place. The journalist in me wanted to chase the lead, to dig deeper, but another part—the part that valued breathing—whispered a name through my panic.

Nate.

My hands shook as I fumbled for my phone, dialing without thinking. It rang once. Twice.

Then, his voice was sharp and gruff. "Whitaker."

I swallowed hard, trying to keep my voice steady. "Nate, it's me." I hesitated, the weight of the note pressing down on my chest. "I... I think I'm in trouble."

His tone changed—hard, focused. "What happened?"

The words tumbled out of me as I clutched the note, my eyes darting across the darkened lot. The silence suddenly felt suffocating.

"Where are you now?" His voice was all business, sharp with urgency.

"The newsroom parking lot." My gaze swept the dimly lit space again, every instinct screaming that I wasn't alone.

"Stay there. I'm on my way." A pause. Then, lower, tighter, "Lock yourself in your car. Don't move."

I nodded before realizing he couldn't see me. "Okay."

My fingers trembled as I hit the lock button, the sharp clunk of the doors sealing me inside barely easing my panic.

I sat stiffly in the driver's seat, breathing shallow as I gripped my phone.

The minutes waiting for Nate to arrive stretched impossibly long.

Finally, headlights pierced the darkness, cutting through the eerie stillness. My breath left me in a sharp exhale as Nate's car pulled next to mine. When I saw his familiar silhouette step out, a flood of relief rushed through me—something I'd never admit out loud.

I pushed open my door and met him halfway, the gravel cold beneath my heels.

His sharp gaze swept over me, his expression unreadable. "You okay?"

I hugged myself, managing a weak nod. "Yeah. Shaken up, but I'll survive." I handed him the note.

Nate's face darkened as he smoothed out the crumpled paper. You need protection, Tessa. I'll have a uniform keeping an eye on you until we track down whoever's behind this."

I scoffed. "Hard pass."

His jaw clenched. "Not up for debate."

"I don't need a damn babysitter following me around, Whitaker," I shot back. "I've got this handled."

"Damn it, Tessa," he snapped, pacing in front of me, his boots grinding against the gravel. "This isn't some game. These people are dangerous. They won't hesitate to—"

"To what?" I challenged, lifting my chin. "To scare me off? To leave me a nasty little warning note? Please. I've dealt with worse."

I saw the muscle in his jaw tick, his frustration rolling off him in waves. The sharp glare of the overhead lights deepened the lines of tension around his mouth, casting his face in sharp, unforgiving angles.

Abruptly, he stopped pacing and turned to me, green eyes blazing. "Fine," he growled. "Since you're too damn stubborn to let one of my officers protect you, that means you're stuck with me."

My stomach flipped. "What?"

"Again, this is not up for debate," he cut in, his tone sharp enough to slice through steel. "Your article kicked the hornet's nest, and now you're standing right in the middle of it. And I'm not letting you get yourself killed."

He stepped in, close enough that I had to tilt my head to meet his eyes. The heat between us crackled like a live wire, but there was no mistaking the determination in his expression.

"If that means camping out at your place 24/7, so be it."

I swallowed hard, pulse hammering.

I should've argued. Should've told him to back off.

But deep down, despite everything, despite the stubborn part of me that hated being told what to do...

I didn't want him to go anywhere.

"Nate, I..." The words caught in my throat as I met his unrelenting stare.

"Save it," he muttered, his voice a low rasp. "Until we sort this out, you're staying where I can see you."

A sharp laugh escaped me, though there was no humor behind it. "Oh really? And what's your grand plan here? Because last I checked, my townhouse isn't exactly set up for unexpected houseguests."

His jaw flexed, his green eyes darkening. "Fine," he said, his voice even lower now. "Then you're coming home with me."

I blinked. "Excuse me?"

Before I could lodge a real protest, Nate's hand settled at the small of my back, guiding me toward his car with a quiet but undeniable authority. A shiver shot straight up my spine at the heat of his touch, even through the fabric of my blouse.

"We'll stop by your place," he continued, his voice gruff but controlled. "You'll pack a bag. And until this blows over, you're staying at my place."

My pulse kicked up at the firm finality in his tone. Part of me wanted to argue, to push back just on principle—but another part, the part still rattled from that damn note, knew better.

We reached his car, and Nate pulled open the passenger door. I glanced up at him, arching a brow. "I can drive myself, you know."

His jaw tightened, his fingers twitching at his side like he had to resist the urge to physically put me in the seat. "Humor me," he murmured, his voice rougher now. "I'll feel better if I can keep an eye on you. I'll have an officer bring your car over later."

I swallowed hard, my heartbeat a traitorous drum against my ribs.

I wasn't entirely sure I wanted to fight him on this.

Chapter Four

♥

NATE

The drive to Tessa's townhouse stretched in tense silence. My grip on the wheel was iron-tight, my jaw locked so hard it ached. Every part of me was still wired from that damn note—its implication, the threat it carried. I didn't like it. I didn't like any of this.

I caught Tessa sneaking glances at me out of the corner of my eye, but I didn't acknowledge them. She was probably plotting how to argue her way out of this, and I didn't have the patience.

When we reached her place, I cut the engine and followed her inside without discussion. She shot me a look but didn't protest—probably realizing it would be pointless.

"Pack enough for a few days," I instructed, crossing my arms as she threw clothes into a bag.

I leaned against the doorframe, watching her move around the room with sharp, deliberate motions. Her silence wasn't compliance—it was restraint. Tessa Donovan didn't back down easily, which meant she was just waiting for the right moment to challenge me.

She yanked the zipper on her bag with more force than necessary and turned, brushing past me without a word. I followed her out, locking the door behind us, my senses still on high alert.

The engine's low drone filled the car, hanging heavy between us like a storm about to break. Her anger was almost tangible, prickling against my already-shot nerves.

She lasted all of thirty seconds.

"This is ridiculous," she snapped, twisting in her seat to face me. "I'm not some kid who needs watching."

I gripped the steering wheel tighter, focusing on the asphalt ahead. "Being capable isn't the point, Tessa. These aren't normal criminals we're dealing with. I won't risk anything happening to you."

Her sigh was long and drawn out, but I wasn't finished.

"You're now a witness in an ongoing investigation," I added, voice steady, firm. "That makes it my job to protect you."

Tessa let her head fall back against the seat, exhaling sharply. "And how long do you expect this arrangement to last?"

"As long as it needs to," I answered without hesitation.

By the time we pulled up to my house, the tension between us had shifted—less sharp, more uncertain.

I led her inside, flicking on the lights. My place was simple, clean, structured. The kind of space that didn't invite company, and yet, here she was, stepping into the one part of my life I'd kept off-limits.

Tessa's gaze swept the living room—leather couch, mounted TV, nothing personal except the few photos on the mantle. I caught her eyes lingering on one: me standing beside my little sister Sophie at her med school graduation, her white coat crisp, my arm slung loosely around her shoulders. She was beaming. I... well, I looked like I wasn't sure what to do with myself.

"Guest room's down the hall on the right," I said, nodding toward it. "Bathroom's across from it. Make yourself at home."

She hesitated, shifting slightly like she wasn't sure what to do with herself. I should've let her go. Should've turned away.

But I didn't.

Instead, I caught her arm before she could disappear down the hall.

"Tessa." My voice came out rougher than I intended like I had to force the words.

She looked up, her breath catching, and damn it, I felt it too—the pull, the weight of something unspoken pressing between us.

"These people don't mess around," I said quietly. "Cross them, and they'll make you disappear."

"I know." Her voice was just as quiet, her gaze steady. "But I can't let this story go."

I moved closer, my body reacting before my brain could shut it down. "I get that," I murmured, my fingers flexing against her arm. "But promise me you won't do anything reckless. No sneaking off, no chasing leads alone. If you find something, you come to me first. Deal?"

Tessa hesitated, and I could see the battle waging in her eyes—journalist instincts versus common sense.

For once, I needed her to choose the latter.

My hand moved on its own, rising to cup her cheek, my thumb grazing the soft curve of her jaw. She sucked in a sharp breath at the contact, her body leaning into mine like she was just as caught in this as I was.

Tension crackled between us, thick and charged, as if the universe was holding its breath, waiting to see what happened next. I didn't know who moved first—maybe it was her, perhaps it was me—but the second our lips met, the last thread of restraint snapped.

A low groan rumbled from my chest as I deepened the kiss, my fingers sliding into her hair, tugging just enough to feel the way she shivered against me. She tasted like trouble, like temptation—like everything I'd spent years convincing myself I didn't want.

And yet, here I was, pulling her closer, kissing her like I'd been starving for her, which I had been.

Tessa melted into me, her arms sliding around my neck, her body pressing against mine like she belonged there. I gripped her waist, pulling her even closer, deepening the kiss with a hunger that had been clawing at me from the moment I met her.

The second my tongue slid against hers, tasting, exploring, I felt her body tense before she let out the softest gasp—one that sent a jolt of heat straight through me.

I lost control.

Pinning her against the wall, I pressed into her, letting her feel exactly what she did to me. My mouth broke from hers, trailing along her jaw, then lower, teeth grazing the sensitive skin beneath her ear. Tessa shuddered, tilting her head back in silent invitation, her nails dragging down my back in a way that made my blood burn.

"Nate," she breathed, arching into me, her fingers tangling in my hair as I sucked at the pulse hammering beneath her skin.

A low growl rumbled from my chest. I gripped her hips tighter, pulling her flush against me, needing more—needing *everything*. When she rocked against me, my restraint cracked, a sharp groan escaping as I crushed my mouth back to hers.

The kiss turned desperate and wild, a clash of heat and need. She tugged at my shirt, her fingers sliding against my skin, lighting every nerve on fire.

This was dangerous.

I knew it.

And I didn't care.

I tore my mouth from hers just long enough to yank my shirt over my head, and then I kissed her again—deep, consuming.

My hands slid beneath her shirt, fingers tracing the dip of her waist, feeling the way she trembled under my touch. I wanted more. Needed more.

Slowly, I worked open each button, my breath turning ragged as the fabric slid from her shoulders, revealing smooth skin and delicate black silk.

"God, look at you," I murmured, my voice rough, eyes drinking her in like she was the only thing that had ever mattered.

A flush crept up her neck, but she didn't shy away. Instead, her fingers moved to the clasp of her bra, unhooking it with a slow, deliberate movement. The silk slipped from her skin, and I sucked in a sharp breath, my restraint hanging by a thread.

My hands found her, cupping her soft curves, thumbs sweeping over her hardened nipples. A shudder ran through her, her breath catching as she arched into my touch, her body fitting perfectly against me.

Mine.

I barely recognized the possessive thought before my lips were on her again, tasting, devouring, chasing the fire.

I dipped my head, replacing my fingers with my mouth, my tongue circling a nipple before pulling it between my lips. She gasped, her back arching as pleasure rippled through her.

"Bed. Now." The words were more command than suggestion.

I lifted her quickly, her legs wrapping around my waist. Our mouths stayed fused, hands grasping, bodies pressed so tight I could feel every shuddered breath against my skin.

We tumbled onto the bed in a heated blur, tangled in each other. My mouth traced the curve of her neck, the delicate line of her collarbone, as my fingers made quick work of the button on her pants. She arched her hips, helping me slide the denim down her legs, and when I pulled back to take her in, my breath damn near left my lungs.

Tessa sprawled across my bed, nothing but a scrap of silk between her and me. Flushed skin, heaving chest, the way she looked up at me—part temptation, part challenge, like she knew exactly what she was doing to me.

"You are so damn beautiful." My voice came out rough, thick with need.

Her fingers trailed down my chest, tracing every ridge, every scar, exploring like she wanted to memorize me. Then she reached my belt, her gaze never wavering as she worked the buckle open, the quiet click sounding impossibly loud in the charged silence.

Her hands moved to my zipper, dragging it down at an agonizing pace, her fingers grazing me through the fabric. My muscles locked, a sharp breath hissing between my teeth.

Tessa smiled before hooking her fingers into my belt loops and dragging my jeans and boxers down. I lifted just enough to help her, heat flaring at every slow caress of her palms over my thighs.

I reached toward the nightstand, fumbling in the drawer momentarily before retrieving a foil packet. My hands trembled slightly as I tore it open, the crinkle of the wrapper loud in the heated silence between us.

Tessa's eyes were drawn to my impressive length as I rolled the condom on with practiced movements.

Tessa pushed me onto my back, straddling my hips as she gazed down at me. Her long dark hair fell in waves around her shoulders, tickling my chest as she leaned forward to capture my lips in a searing kiss. My hands roamed up her thighs to grip her waist, steadying her as she positioned herself above me.

Tessa sank down slowly, taking me deep inside her. She was tight and hot around me, a perfect fit. I gripped her hips, guiding her movements as she began to rock against me.

"God, Tessa," I groaned. "You feel perfect. So tight, hot, and wet."

She began to move, rolling her hips in a slow, torturous rhythm. I met her movements, thrusting up as she came down. The friction was exquisite, sending waves of pleasure through my body. Tessa's head fell back, exposing the elegant line of her throat as she rode me.

My hands roamed her body, caressing her breasts, her waist, her thighs. I couldn't get enough of her silky skin under my palms.

Tessa's pace quickened, her movements becoming more urgent as pleasure built between us. I gripped her hips tighter, guiding her into a faster rhythm. She braced her hands on my chest, nails digging in slightly as she ground against me.

"Nate," she moaned, her voice breathy and desperate.

I could feel her trembling so close to the edge. I slid a hand between our bodies, my thumb finding her sensitive bundle of nerves. She cried out at the added stimulation, her inner walls clenching around me.

"Fuck," she gasped, her nails raking down my chest. "Oh god, yes..."

Tessa's movements grew more frantic. I thrust up to meet her, driving deeper with each stroke. My thumb circled her clit relentlessly as I felt her start to tighten around me.

"Oh god, Nate," she moaned. "I'm so close..."

I thrust up harder to meet her, my hand gripping her hip tightly. "Fucking come for me, Tessa," I demanded roughly. "Let me feel you."

With a cry of pleasure, she shattered above me. Her body arched as waves of ecstasy washed over her. The sight of her coming undone pushed me over the edge, and I followed right after, groaning her name as intense pleasure pulsed through me.

We clung to each other as pleasure rippled through us, our ragged breaths filling the quiet. Tessa sank against my chest, spent and boneless.

As I came down from the high, reality started to take over. My body went still as the weight of what we'd just done settled over me like a lead blanket. Guilt churned in my gut, warring with the raw, undeniable need to pull Tessa closer, to keep her tangled in my arms and forget everything else.

But I couldn't.

I exhaled sharply, forcing myself to move, untangle from her body's warmth. She stirred, making a quiet sound of protest, her fingers brushing against my arm as if reaching for me. My chest clenched at the simple, unconscious gesture.

I ignored it. Ignored the pull to stay.

Sliding out of bed, I disposed of the condom before reaching for my boxers. When I turned back, Tessa watched me, her blue eyes still hazy from lust, a lazy smile teasing her lips. And damn it, the sight sent something sharp and dangerous through me.

"Tessa, I…" I ran a hand through my hair, searching for words I didn't want to say. "This was a mistake."

The smile vanished. Hurt flickered across her face before she masked it, locking her expression into something unreadable. "A mistake?" she repeated, her voice too neutral, too controlled.

I sighed, reaching for my jeans. "We can't do this," I muttered, not trusting myself to look at her. "It's too complicated."

Tessa sat up slowly, pulling the sheet around her like armor. Her eyes were sharper now, any trace of softness replaced with something harder. "Too complicated?" she echoed, her tone like a blade. "That's quite a shift from a few minutes ago when you couldn't keep your hands off me."

My jaw clenched as I buttoned my jeans. "I got caught up in the moment," I said, forcing steel into my voice. "But it can't happen again."

"Why not?" she demanded, gripping the sheet tighter as she stood. "Because I'm a journalist? Because I'm involved in your case?"

"Yes and yes." The words came out harsher than I intended, but I didn't take them back. My hands curled into fists at my sides as I met her glare head-on. "Damn it, Tessa, you're a witness now."

Her eyes flashed, anger sparking beneath the hurt. "So that's it? We sleep together, and now you're just going to push me away?"

I dragged a hand down my face, my frustration mounting. "It's not that simple."

"It is that simple, Nate."

"No, it's not." My voice was sharp, cutting through the tension between us. "You're involved in an active investigation. There are ethical considerations, professional boundaries—"

"Oh, please," she scoffed, crossing her arms, the sheet slipping slightly as she glared at me. "Don't hide behind your badge. This isn't about ethics, and you know it. This is about you being afraid."

I stiffened, something inside me snapping. "Afraid?" The word came out like a challenge. "I'm trying to protect you. And my damn case. If anyone finds out about this, it could compromise everything."

Tessa let out a hollow laugh, shaking her head. "So I'm just a liability to you now?" Her voice wavered slightly, cutting deeper than I wanted to admit. She clutched the sheet closer, looking more exposed than I'd ever seen her.

I should've said something. Should've fixed it. Instead, I let the silence stretch between us, thick with everything I wanted but couldn't have.

Moonlight spilled through the window, casting silver over her skin and highlighting every curve beneath the thin sheet she clutched around her body. Her dark hair tumbled over her shoulders in wild waves, a stark contrast to the guarded expression on her face. And despite everything—the fight, the regret, the damn wall I was trying to build between us—I couldn't stop wanting her.

I clenched my jaw, shoving the thought away. Focus. Control.

I dragged a hand down my face and exhaled sharply. "It's late," I said, trying to remain in control. "We're both exhausted. Everything's too raw right now. Let's just get some sleep. We'll figure this out in the morning."

Tessa's lips pressed into a firm line. Her posture screamed resistance like she wanted to argue, to tell me exactly how full of shit I was. But after a long pause, she just nodded, stiff and silent.

I caught the slight movement of her throat as she swallowed hard like she was forcing herself not to say something she'd regret. The weight of the moment settled between us—thick, charged, tangled with words left unsaid.

Tessa turned away first. The soft rustle of fabric filled the room as she gathered her clothes, the sound unnervingly loud in the quiet. She didn't look at me as she slipped past, her bare feet silent against the hardwood.

I let her go.

Didn't stop her. Didn't say another word.

I just stood there, fists clenched, staring at the empty space she left behind—hating how much I wanted to go after her.

Chapter Five

♥

TESSA

The door clicked shut behind me, the soft sound somehow deafening in the quiet. I leaned against it, pressing my forehead against the cool wood, trying to steady my breath. My fingers trembled as I finally let go of the sheet, letting it slip to the floor in a heap at my feet.

Moonlight streamed through the gossamer curtains, casting soft silver light across the blue walls. The queen-sized bed sat in the center of the room, perfectly made, untouched. It looked too pristine—and far too empty. I moved to the dresser, setting down the bundle of hastily gathered clothes, but my eyes caught my reflection in the mirror before me.

My skin was still flushed, my lips swollen from Nate's kisses. My fingers drifted to my collarbone, brushing over where his mouth had lingered, sending a shiver racing down my spine.

Damn him.

With a sharp exhale, I turned away, pacing the length of the room, my bare feet sinking into the plush rug. My thoughts spun wildly, frustration curling through me. He could pretend all he wanted that this was a mistake and didn't mean anything—but I knew better. The way he touched me, kissed me—that wasn't something you walked away from so easily.

I wasn't about to let Nate Whitaker's fear of emotions dictate what this was between us.

Sinking onto the edge of the bed, I ran my hands over the soft cotton sheets—expensive, high thread count, a surprising contrast to the no-nonsense detective who slept in this house. The scent of fresh linen mixed with something distinctly Nate—woodsy, warm, a smell I was already craving again.

Lying back against the pillows, I stared at the ceiling, watching shadows shift in the dim light. No matter how much I tried to push it away, the memories crept back in—his hands on my skin, his mouth at my ear, the deep, gravelly way he said my name when he lost himself in me.

My thighs clenched instinctively, a slow burn pooling low in my belly.

A quiet, frustrated sigh slipped past my lips. Damn him. Again.

I could go back to him. I could walk down the hall, crawl back into his bed, press my body against his, and make him forget every damn excuse he thought he had. I could remind him, without a single word, how impossible it was to fight this.

But I wouldn't.

I wasn't the kind of woman who begged.

So instead, I curled onto my side, gripping a pillow that faintly smelled of him, and forced myself to close my eyes. Sleep came in fits, filled with restless dreams of Nate's touch, his voice, and the way his body fit so perfectly against mine.

The scent of coffee pulled me awake far too soon. Blinking against the soft morning light, I took in the unfamiliar room.

Then it hit me.

Nate. Last night. His hands, his mouth. The way he'd looked at me.

Frustration curled through me as I sat up, rubbing a hand over my face. I wasn't ready to face him, not yet.

But ready or not, I had no choice.

I got dressed and went out to face him, face this.

Morning sunlight sliced through the kitchen blinds, casting sharp golden streaks across the countertops. Nate stood at the coffee maker, gripping the counter like it was the only thing keeping him upright. His broad shoulders were tense, his jaw locked, and when I stepped into the room, his body stiffened even more.

"Morning," I said carefully, watching him.

His eyes flicked toward me, then away, as he muttered, "Morning." He poured two mugs of coffee, setting one on the table without looking at me.

I grabbed the coffee cup but didn't sit. "So, what's the plan?" I asked, crossing my arms. "Are we just going to pretend last night didn't happen?"

His shoulders went even stiffer.

"There's nothing to talk about," he said, voice clipped.

I scoffed, shaking my head. "Nothing to talk about? Nate, I'm staying in your house because someone threatened me over an article I wrote. And last night—"

"Last night shouldn't have happened," he cut in, turning just enough for me to see the storm brewing in his green eyes. "I let things get too personal."

Something sharp lodged itself in my throat. My fingers tightened around the coffee mug, heat seeping into my skin. "Too personal?" My voice rose, disbelief laced through every word. "What the hell does that even mean?"

He exhaled sharply, finally facing me fully, his frustration simmering just beneath the surface. "It means I can't do this. I can't give you what you're looking for."

I froze. My pulse pounded in my ears. "What I'm looking for?" I repeated, my breath catching. "I didn't ask for anything, Nate."

"Not yet," he muttered, raking a hand through his messy hair. "And that's the problem." His eyes locked onto mine, intense, conflicted. "You deserve someone who can give you everything—commitment, stability, a future." His voice dropped. "I'm not that guy."

The words landed like a gut punch, knocking the air out of me. I forced myself to hold his gaze, even as my heart twisted painfully in my chest.

I slammed the coffee mug onto the table, the sharp *clack* cutting through the heavy silence. My pulse pounded, my breath coming fast as I glared at Nate. "Stop pretending this is about me when we both know it's about you. It's about you and whatever ghosts you're still carrying. You're scared, plain and simple."

Nate's mug hit the counter with a force that rattled the dishes in the sink. "This isn't about fear, damn it! You deserve better than what I've got to offer."

I stormed forward, stepping right into his space, my chest brushing his as I tipped my chin to meet his furious gaze. "Save the martyr routine. I don't need you playing guardian over my life choices. I know exactly what I want, and it's standing right in front of me, making excuses. You're just too *chickenshit* to face it."

His jaw clenched, his breathing ragged. "Chickenshit?" His voice dropped to a low, dangerous whisper. "You think I'm chickenshit because I don't want to drag you into my mess? Because I don't want to make promises, I can't keep?"

"No," I fired back, my voice shaking with anger. "I think you're a chickenshit because you'd rather push me away than risk letting me in. Because you'd rather stay miserable and alone than take a damn chance."

His whole body tensed like I'd landed a punch. The air between us crackled, thick with tension, and Nate turned away, his fists clenching at his sides.

"This is for the best," he muttered, his voice raw.

A sharp sting bloomed in my chest, stealing my breath for a second before I swallowed it down. "Best for who?" My voice wavered, but I forced steel into it. "Because it sure as hell isn't *best* for me."

Nate flinched but didn't turn around. That was all the answer I needed.

I let out a harsh laugh, shaking my head. "You know what, Nate? You're right. I *do* deserve more. More than empty promises. More than being treated like an inconvenience." I grabbed my bag from the couch, my movements stiff and controlled. "If you can't step up, fine. But don't pretend walking away makes you the good guy here."

Still, nothing. Not a single word.

I stared at his rigid back, my chest aching, hoping—*praying*—for something. Anything. A reason to stay.

But the silence between us hung heavy, suffocating, and finally, the last thread of hope snapped.

I exhaled slowly, my voice trembling but sure as I said, "I deserve better than this. And if you're too blind to see it, then you never deserved me."

Then I turned and walked out, leaving Nate Whitaker standing in the wreckage of what could have been.

NATE

The front door slammed behind her, the sound ricocheting through the hollow quiet of my house. My fingers dug into the kitchen counter, my breath coming fast, uneven. My eyes landed on her half-finished coffee mug, the ceramic still warm from where her lips had touched it.

She was gone.

The silence she left behind settled over me like a damn weight, pressing into my ribs, suffocating. I'd told myself for years that solitude was safety. That it was better to be alone than to risk losing something—someone—again.

But for the first time, I realized how much of a lie that was. Because this? This wasn't safety. It was hell.

I shoved a hand through my hair, forcing my thoughts to sharpen. No matter how pissed she was, no matter how much she wanted to cut ties, Tessa was still in danger. And I wasn't about to let her walk away without protection.

Pulling my phone from my pocket, I dialed dispatch, my voice rough as I forced out the order. "I need a uniform stationed near Tessa Donovan's place. Unmarked car. No lights, no sirens. Just keep an eye on her."

"Copy that, Detective," the officer on duty confirmed.

I exhaled, tension gripping my spine. It wasn't enough—I wanted to be the one watching over her, the one keeping her safe—but I'd lost that right the second I let her walk out the door.

Jaw clenched, I pushed away from the counter, shoving every thought of Tessa aside the only way I knew how—by drowning myself in work.

***

The next few weeks were a blur of evidence files, caffeine, and long nights spent chasing leads that had eluded me for months. I spent hours untangling the web of lies Rick Hayes had spun—layer after layer of shell companies, fake accounts, and orchestrated distractions that had kept his real crimes hidden in plain sight.

But I wasn't the kind of detective who gave up when things got messy. And the deeper I dug, the clearer the picture became.

The break-ins and robberies weren't just random hits—they were calculated. A smokescreen to mask a bigger play. Hayes wasn't just stirring up chaos; he was part of a push to drive local businesses out, making it easier for developers to swoop in and take over. Every robbery, every act of vandalism, it all served the same purpose—forcing the owners to their breaking point until they had no choice but to sell.

And now, I finally had enough to nail the slimy bastard.

But, the satisfaction I expected from taking Hayes down never came.

Because this wasn't just my win.

Tessa should've been here.

Her work had cracked this case open, giving me the leads I needed to bring Hayes down. This was *her* story. And I'd shoved her out of it, out of *my* life.

I'd convinced myself it was for the best.

So why did it feel like I'd just lost the most important thing of all?

I grabbed my phone, my thumb hovering over her name, the screen casting a faint glow in the dark cab of my truck. Every instinct screamed at me to press call, to tell her everything—to say the words I should have said that night instead of shoving her away.

But then I remembered her face when she left. How the light in her eyes had dimmed, how she had looked at me like she finally saw me for the coward I was. I'd told myself pushing her away was the right thing, the noble thing. But sitting here now, drowning in silence, that felt like a joke.

With a sharp curse, I shoved the phone back into my pocket and gripped the wheel.

Then I drove.

I had no destination in mind; I just let my hands steer on autopilot through the familiar streets of Anchor Bay. The streetlights blurred past, and my thoughts tangled with every moment I'd spent with her—every argument, every sharp-witted comeback, every stolen second where I let myself want her.

The truck slowed, and I parked outside her building before registering where I was.

Damn it.

I sat there, engine idling, staring at the soft glow from her window. My pulse hammered, and my breath became shallow. I had no plan, no speech prepared—just the undeniable pull to see her, to fix what I had broken between us.

Then, the front door swung open.

I stilled.

Not Tessa.

A man.

Tall. Confident. A face I recognized instantly.

Ryan Anderson.

Search and Rescue specialist. Worked on a few cases with us. Good instincts. Steady hands. The kind of guy who didn't rattle easy.

And right now, he was standing too damn close to Tessa.

Her hair tumbled over her shoulder, catching the streetlamp's glow, and those striking blue eyes shone as she looked up at *him*. She said something, and Ryan laughed—an easy, familiar laugh that twisted my stomach.

Then she smiled.

A genuine, easy, *happy* smile. The kind I hadn't seen in weeks. The kind that used to be *mine*.

Ryan leaned against the railing, relaxed, too comfortable in her space. Tessa laughed again, and I felt like the wind was knocked out of me.

My hands clenched around the wheel, my heart pounding in a way I hated.

I should leave. I had no right to be here, no claim to her, not after what I did.

But I couldn't look away.

Not when she was standing there, looking at another man the way I wanted her to look at *me*.

I couldn't hear what they said, but I didn't need to. The way she smiled at him, the way she leaned in just slightly—it was enough.

Tessa didn't need me to complicate her life. She deserved better. Someone like Ryan—charming, confident, probably not carrying a damn freight train of baggage everywhere he went.

My grip tightened on the wheel as I fought the urge to get out of the truck, cut into their conversation, and *do something*. But what the hell would I even say? That I was sorry? That I didn't mean it when I said we wouldn't work? That I had spent every single night since pushing her away regretting it?

Would it even matter?

My jaw locked as I forced my hands to move, shifting the truck into gear. I didn't let myself hesitate, didn't let myself look at her one last time as I pulled away from the curb.

Because if I did, I might not have been able to leave.

And as the distance grew between us, the weight in my chest only got heavier.

I had lost her.

Chapter Six

♥

TESSA

The familiar hum of my laptop filled my townhouse as I sat at my desk, its glow casting flickering shadows on the walls. My fingers hovered uselessly over the keyboard, the title of my next article blinking at the top of a blank document:

Into the Storm: The High-Stakes World of Search and Rescue Specialist Ryan Anderson.

The words blurred. My recorder sat beside me, filled with snippets from my earlier interview. Ryan had been easy to talk to—charming, insightful, the kind of guy who made you forget the world around you when he spoke. His stories about rescues in impossible conditions, the razor-thin line between life and death, the ones he saved and the ones he couldn't—had drawn me in.

It should have had my full attention. It was precisely the kind of piece I loved writing, the kind of story that reminded me why I did this in the first place.

And yet... my fingers remained still.

Because instead of focusing on Ryan, my mind kept drifting to Nate.

I let out a frustrated sigh, leaning back in my chair as I rubbed my temples. No matter how hard I tried to shove him from my thoughts, he was still there—lurking like a shadow, unshakable.

The way his presence filled a room before he even spoke.

The rough edge of his voice when he was frustrated with me and the rare softness when he wasn't.

I squeezed my eyes shut. *Enough.*

I had spent too much time trying to crack the mystery that was Nate Whitaker, trying to understand what made him pull me in one second and shove me away the next. He was a lost cause—too closed off, too consumed by the ghosts he refused to shake.

And yet...

My gaze dropped to the recorder, and for a moment, I wished it held *his* voice instead of Ryan's. That gruff, no-nonsense tone lecturing me about safety, about being reckless, about making his life harder than it needed to be. Because beneath all of that irritation, there had always been something else. Something raw, real.

I swallowed against the lump in my throat, sitting up straighter.

"This is ridiculous," I muttered. "Pull yourself together, Tessa."

I wasn't some lovesick fool. I had a career, a life, a damn good story waiting to be written.

I just had to stop wanting *him* more than all of it.

I slumped back in my chair, rubbing my hands over my face. No point in pretending I could focus. That hollow ache in my chest wasn't going anywhere.

Then it hit me—sudden, sharp, impossible to ignore.

If Nate Whitaker thought he could push me away that easily, he was about to learn just how wrong he was.

I slammed my laptop shut, pushing my chair back with a scrape of wood against the floor. My keys were in my hand before I'd even registered grabbing them, my heart pounding as I snatched my jacket and bolted for the door.

I swung open the door and there he was.

Disheveled. Exhausted.

Nate stood in the doorway, his hair sticking up at odd angles like he'd been raking his fingers through it for hours.

His mouth opened, then shut again. For a man who always had a sharp retort or a gruff command, he suddenly looked like he had no idea what to say.

"Tessa," he finally croaked out, voice rough like gravel. "We need to talk. Really talk."

I stepped back to let him in and as he walked past me the scent of coffee and something undeniably *him* wrapped around me.

I turned to face him as I shut the door, forcing myself to meet his gaze head-on.

"You're right." His voice barely rose above a whisper, but the confession hung heavy between us. "I am scared. Terrified, actually."

My breath caught as something inside him cracked. The ever-controlled, ever-guarded detective wasn't standing in front of me anymore. Instead, I saw the man beneath the armor—the one who had been fighting this war alone for far too long.

"I'm terrified," he admitted, his voice breaking. "Terrified of how much I want you. How much I *need* you."

He paced across the room like he could outrun the emotions clawing their way to the surface.

"I've spent years building these walls, keeping everyone at arm's length. It was easier that way—safer. But then *you* came along, crashing into my life with your determination, fearlessness, and beautiful smile."

I sucked in a breath as he took a step closer. Close enough that I could see the flicker of gold in his green eyes, the raw intensity burning behind them.

"I told myself I was protecting you by pushing you away," he murmured. "But the truth? I was protecting *myself*."

His voice turned rough, filled with something dark and aching. "Because letting you in, opening myself up again... it *terrifies* me. And, I don't know if I can do it, if I'm strong enough."

Nate's voice was raw, thick with emotion. "But watching you walk away that day... God, Tessa, it felt like my heart was ripped from my chest. And I realized that the pain of losing you was far worse than any fear I had about letting you in."

My heart clenched at the sheer honesty in his words. I reached for him without thinking, my fingers brushing down his arm until they found his hand.

"Nate," I said softly, lacing my fingers with his. "I'm scared too. This thing between us... it's intense and overwhelming and, yeah, terrifying. But that doesn't mean it's not worth fighting for."

His grip tightened, and his green eyes searched mine, full of hesitation. "What if I mess this up?" he murmured. "What if I hurt you?"

I squeezed his hand, holding on as if I could physically anchor him to me. "What if you don't?" I countered. "What if this is something amazing, and we miss out because we're too afraid to try?"

I stepped closer, feeling the warmth radiating from him, the heat that had always existed between us. "I can't promise we won't hurt each other, Nate. That's part of opening yourself up, of letting someone in. But I *can* promise that it's worth the risk."

A breath shuddered out of him as he reached up, his hand cupping my cheek. His thumb brushed over my skin in a touch so gentle and reverent that it nearly undid me.

"You deserve so much better than a broken man with more baggage than the airport lost and found," he whispered, his voice rough, his gaze tortured.

I looked up at him, my chest tightening, but my voice was steady when I answered. "We *all* have baggage, Nate. What matters is finding someone willing to help you carry it."

His breath hitched, his fingers tensing against my skin. I could see the war in his eyes, the push and pull of every doubt and every longing.

"Tessa, I—"

I didn't let him finish. I rose onto my toes, closed the space between us, and kissed him. Not like before, not the way we had in moments of heat and reckless passion. This was softer, slower—an offering. A promise.

For a single beat, he didn't move. Then, with a quiet, almost defeated sigh, his arms wrapped around me, pulling me against him like he'd never let go.

"I love you," he murmured against my lips, the words breathless, like they'd been locked inside him for too long. "Have since you walked into my crime scene, if I'm being honest."

A laugh bubbled out of me, and I pulled back just enough to meet his gaze, my heart swelling. "I love you too," I admitted, the truth settling deep in my bones. "God, I've been sitting on those words for weeks."

Nate's eyes darkened as he gazed down at me, his hands sliding to my hips. "Let me show you how much I love you," he murmured, his voice low and husky.

He guided me backward until my legs hit the couch. I sank onto the soft fabric, my breath catching as Nate knelt before me. His strong hands caressed up my thighs, pushing my skirt higher.

"I've wanted to taste you for days, weeks," he said, his eyes never leaving mine.

I moaned, unable to find my voice as desire pooled low in my belly. Nate's fingers hooked into my panties, slowly sliding them down my legs. The cool air hit my heated skin, making me shiver.

Nate's hands pushed my legs apart gently, his thumbs tracing teasing circles on my inner thighs.

I trembled, anticipation building as he worked his way higher. When his tongue finally flicked against my sensitive flesh, I gasped, my hips bucking involuntarily.

"God, Tessa," he groaned. "You taste so fucking good."

He licked a long, slow stripe up my slit before focusing his attention on my clit. My fingers tangled in his hair as pleasure rippled through me. Nate's tongue circled and flicked relentlessly, stoking the fire building inside me.

"Nate," I panted. "Oh god, don't stop."

He slid two fingers inside me, curling them as he pumped in and out. His tongue circled my clit again before sucking gently, drawing another low moan from my throat.

Nate's fingers pumped in and out as his tongue worked magic on my clit. Pleasure built rapidly, coiling tighter and tighter in my core. My thighs trembled around his head as I got closer to the edge.

"I've thought about this, Nate," I gasped out, about to come faster than I ever had in my life. "But this is so much better than I even imagined."

Nate groaned against me, the vibrations sending shockwaves of pleasure through my body. He pulled back just enough to look up at me, his eyes dark with desire.

"God, Tessa," he rasped, his voice rough with need. "I've thought about this too. Every damn night since you walked out that door."

His fingers continued their relentless rhythm inside me as he spoke, his thumb now circling my clit.

"I'd lie in bed, picturing you just like this," he admitted, his gaze burning into mine. "Spread out for me, trembling under my touch. I'd stroke myself, imagining it was your hand, your mouth."

A shudder ran through me at his words, heat coiling tighter in my core. Nate's eyes never left mine as he lowered his head again, his tongue resuming its torturous assault on my clit.

At his admission, a surge of heat rushed through me. The image of Nate lying in bed, stroking himself while thinking of me, sent my arousal skyrocketing. His fingers curled inside me, hitting that perfect spot as his tongue flicked rapidly over my swollen clit.

"Oh god, Nate!" I cried out, my back arching off the couch.

The coil of pleasure inside me snapped, and I came hard, waves of intense ecstasy crashing over me. My inner walls clenched rhythmically around his fingers as he worked me through my orgasm. My thighs trembled uncontrollably, my fingers tightening in his hair as I rode out the sensations.

As I came down from the high, my body boneless and spent, Nate pressed soft kisses to my inner thighs. He looked up at me, his eyes dark with desire, his lips glistening.

Something fierce and possessive flashed in his eyes as he rose up, his mouth capturing mine in a kiss that stole my breath. I tasted myself on his lips, and it only heightened my desire.

Nate cupped my face, his thumb tracing along my cheek, his gaze burning into mine. "I love you, Tessa Donovan," he said, his voice rough with conviction. "And this? Us? It's not just some fleeting thing. This is only the beginning. I'm not letting fear, my past, or my own damn stubbornness stand in the way anymore. I will prove to you every day that I love you—that you're it for me."

My lips curled into a slow, teasing smile as I ran my fingers over his jaw. "Well," I murmured, my eyes glinting with mischief, "I'd say that was a pretty damn good start."

Nate huffed out a laugh, shaking his head as he pulled me closer. "You're impossible."

"And you love it," I shot back, looping my arms around his neck.

His grin softened as he brushed his lips over mine. "Yeah," he admitted, pressing his forehead to mine. "I really, really do."

Epilogue

♥

NATE

I used to think love wasn't for me. Hell, I knew it wasn't for me.

I'd walked through the wreckage of a failed marriage, picked up the pieces of a life I thought I was building, only to realize I'd been standing on quicksand the whole time. So I made a choice—never again. Never again would I put myself in a position where someone could walk away and take everything with them.

And then Tessa stormed into my life.

Sharp wit. Relentless determination. That damn ability to see right through me.

I should've kept my distance. I should've walked away.

But loving Tessa was never a choice.

It was inevitable.

She hadn't just knocked down my walls—she'd walked right through them like they were never there in the first place. And somehow, I wasn't mad about it.

The clink of glasses and low hum of conversation at *The Rusty Anchor* pulled me from my thoughts. Across the table, Tessa lifted her drink, amusement flickering in her eyes.

"Detective Whitaker," she teased, smirking. "You're staring."

I huffed a quiet laugh, shaking my head as I took a sip of my beer. "Maybe I like what I see."

Her brows lifted in mock surprise. "Careful, Nate. If you keep being this charming, people might start thinking you're not the grumpy, emotionally unavailable detective you pretend to be."

I smirked, reaching beneath the table to squeeze her thigh. "You like my grumpy side."

Tessa's laugh was light, teasing. "I tolerate it."

Bullshit. She loved it.

And I loved her.

The words sat on the tip of my tongue, not because I was afraid to say them, but because I already had. A hundred times over, in every kiss, every argument, in every damn way I'd fought for her since I finally pulled my head out of my ass.

For the first time in a long time, I wasn't looking over my shoulder, waiting for the other shoe to drop. I wasn't bracing for disappointment or failure.

Tessa wasn't my weakness.

She was my strength.

And I'd be damned if I ever let her go.

***

Dear Reader,

Thank you so much for reading *Investigating Desire*! I hope you loved Nate and Tessa's story—their fiery banter, undeniable chemistry, and the push and pull of a connection neither of them expected. Writing their journey was a thrill, and I'm so grateful you came along for the ride.

If you enjoyed the book, I'd truly appreciate it if you took a moment to leave a review. Reviews help authors like me connect with more readers, and even a few words can make a huge difference in sharing these stories.

Thank you for your support—I can't wait to bring you more swoon-worthy, slow-burn romance with plenty of sparks and heat!

With gratitude,Hana York

***

Ready for More?

If you loved *Investigating Desire*, get ready for an action-packed, slow-burn romance in *Falling for the Rescue*!

Ryan Anderson has spent his career pulling people from the brink—calm under pressure, relentless in the field. But when a rescue gone wrong leaves him stranded in the middle of a storm, he finds himself on the other side of the equation. Enter Sam Monroe, an ex-military K9 handler with zero patience for reckless heroes or bruised egos. She's got one job: get Ryan to safety, whether he likes it or not.

Trapped together in a remote cabin as the storm rages, tensions rise, walls crack, and the chemistry between them becomes impossible to ignore. But Ryan isn't used to being the one who needs saving, and Sam has spent too long standing on her own to trust someone to catch her.

Can they weather the storm brewing between them, or will fear and pride keep them from the one thing they never saw coming?

Keep reading for a sneak peek at Falling for the Rescue – Available on Amazon!

Sneak Peak of Falling for the Rescue

❤

RYAN

F rigid rain pierced my skin, soaking through my jacket until I was chilled to the core. One moment, I stood on firm ground, the next—nothing. The earth crumbled beneath me as a cascade of mud ripped my legs out from under me, dragging me down to the bottom of this god-forsaken ravine.

I drew in a sharp breath, my left ankle screaming in protest. Not broken—I'd tested that much—but walking was out of the question. Even worse, my pack had vanished in the chaos.

Grinding my teeth against the frustration bubbling under my skin, I raised my radio. "This is Anderson. I'm stuck in a ravine near marker six. My ankle's injured. I need backup."

Static crackled before the reply came. "Copy that, Anderson. Hold tight. All of our people are tied up, but we have a specialist who is in town for training. I will dispatch them with K9 support to your location."

I exhaled sharply, dragging a hand down my rain-soaked face. "ETA?"

A pause. Then, "As soon as possible. Weather's slowing everything down."

Of course it was.

I shoved my radio back into my vest and leaned against the cold rock face. The downpour was relentless, sheets of rain making everything slick, the ground unstable. I hated waiting. Hated sitting still even more. I wasn't the guy who needed rescuing—I was the one doing the rescuing.

Time crawled by; the only sounds were the storm and the occasional crackle of my radio. Then—something else. Faint but distinct.

Barking.

My head snapped up. I squinted against the rain, scanning the jagged rim of the ravine. A moment later, a voice cut through the storm—sharp, no-nonsense.

"Anderson, you down there?"

"Yeah!" I called back, my pulse kicking up. "About time! You the specialist?"

"Something like that," the voice returned. "Stay put. I'm lowering a harness."

A rope came down with a harness attached. I adjusted my weight, easing the harness over my shoulders and under my legs, wincing as the shift jostled my ankle.

"You good?" The voice came again, firm but focused.

"Yeah, let's do this."

The line went taut, jerking me up inch by painstaking inch. The harness dug into my ribs, the rain-slick rope creaking under the weight.

As I neared the top, I expected a strong, calloused hand to be there—probably attached to some burly guy built like a linebacker.

Instead, I found a lithe figure standing back near the rigging, her stance steady despite the mud and rain. Definitely not what I'd pictured.

Through the dim light, I caught glimpses of the setup—a pulley system secured to a sturdy tree just beyond the ravine's edge. Efficient. Clean. Smart. And the woman handling it? Just as steady and sure as the rigging itself, her gloved hands working with practiced precision to guide me up.

The harness gave one last tug, and suddenly, I was over the edge, sprawled on the slick, uneven ground. Before I could fully process the shift, she was already moving, stepping toward me with sharp, no-nonsense eyes.

That was when I noticed the powerful Chinook dog beside her, muscles taut, standing at attention like he'd been part of the operation the whole time.

Rain slicked off her jacket as she closed the remaining distance, her short brown hair plastered to her forehead.

I exhaled, dragging a hand through my damp hair. "Not gonna lie," I muttered. "Was expecting someone... bigger."

Her lips twitched, but she didn't pause as she crouched next to me, already testing my ankle for damage. "And yet, here you are. Upright. Breathing. Rescued."

I huffed out a breath, still trying to catch up. "Hell of a setup you've got."

She gave a slight nod, all business. "Gets the job done." Then her gaze flicked up to mine, steady and unwavering.

"Sam Monroe, Search and Rescue from Granite Falls." She jerked her chin toward the dog. "That's Chance."

I let out a breath, still catching up to how fast she was moving. "Ryan Anderson. SAR, Anchor Bay—usually on the other end of these things."

Her lips twitched, just barely. "Guess it's your turn to be rescued."

I huffed. "Not my favorite position."

She crouched beside me, running a quick, practiced eye over me. "Right now, I'm worried about you—can you walk?"

I shifted, testing my ankle, and immediately clenched my jaw against the sharp stab of pain. "Not a chance. Ankle's toast."

She sized me up with a calculating look, scanning me from head to toe. "Let me guess—six-four, around two-twenty?"

"Something like that," I grumbled.

"Great," she said, strapping her pack to her dog's harness. "I'll carry you."

My head snapped up. "Wait, what? I don't need you to carry me."

Her jaw tightened. "We're half a click from an abandoned cabin. The storm's getting worse, and I'm not arguing about this."

I opened my mouth to protest, but the glare she shot me was colder than the rain. Before I could get another word out, she crouched and, with surprising ease, hoisted me onto her back.

I let out a stunned breath as she adjusted her grip, her movements smooth and efficient. The Chinook took the lead, guiding us through the uneven terrain like this was just another day at the office.

I couldn't ignore the slight hitch in her step—carrying my weight couldn't have been easy—but she didn't falter. If anything, she moved with a steady determination that left me speechless. And, yeah, more than a little humbled.

"Do this often?" I muttered, my pride taking a hit as I clung to her shoulders.

"More than you'd think," she said, shifting me on her back with an effortlessness that made my ego ache. "Though I usually get fewer complaints and less dead weight."

I huffed a breath against her damp shoulder. "Dead weight? I was trying to make your job easier."

"Uh-huh." Her tone was dry, but I thought she might be smiling. "Keep telling yourself that."

Despite the storm, the pain, and my bruised ego, a low chuckle escaped me. "You don't pull any punches, do you?"

"Not my style," she said, carefully navigating the rocky ground. "Though I'll give you credit—you're easily top three for heaviest rescue."

I lifted a brow. "Top three?" My voice carried mock indignation. "Should I be flattered or offended?"

She smirked, her grip tightening around my legs as she pushed forward. "Let's just say you've made an impression."

SAM

I readjusted Ryan's weight across my shoulders, trying to distribute it more evenly. The rain slammed down, ice-cold and merciless, but I was too focused to care. My eyes stayed fixed on the muddy path ahead, each step measured and deliberate.

I'd hauled heavier bodies through worse terrain before. The mud sucked at my boots like desert sand, each step a fight against the earth itself. My muscles screamed in protest, and my legs burned with a familiar ache. Then the memories hit, uninvited and raw.

Blistering heat, swallowing me whole. The weight of my squadmate over my shoulders, his uniform soaked with blood and sweat. Mortar fire shook the ground, dust clouds swallowing the sky. Every breath clogged my throat with grit. The desperate shouts of my unit rang in my ears, but all I could hear was the thunder of my own pulse. I had to keep moving. Had to get him out.

Ryan shifted slightly against me, and I was yanked back to the present like a slap to the face. Cold rain replaced scorching sun. The only sound was the downpour and our staggered breaths. But my heart was still hammering. My grip on him tightened, but my hands wouldn't stop trembling.

"Sam?" His voice cut through the haze, low and steady. "You good?"

I didn't answer immediately, my jaw locking as I forced myself to keep moving. The cabin wasn't far. Just a few more steps. I could feel Ryan's arm pressing against my shoulder, steady despite the storm, and I knew he could feel the way my pulse was racing.

"Sam," he tried again, softer this time like he already knew. "Your heart's going a mile a minute. Are you—"

"I'm fine." The words snapped out sharper than I intended, but I didn't apologize. If I let him push, if I let myself crack, I wasn't sure I'd be able to put the pieces back together.

And I hated that. Hated that I wasn't holding it together as well as I should have.

The cabin finally loomed ahead, its dark outline cutting through the rain. Relief flared hot in my chest, but the knots in my stomach didn't ease. I couldn't let the past get in my head. Not when I had a job to finish.

I stopped before the porch steps, adjusting my stance before lowering Ryan as carefully as possible. The second his boots hit the ground, I stepped back, rolling my shoulders to shake off the ghost of weight clinging to me.

"This is as far as I can carry you," I said, brushing damp hair from my face. My voice was steady now. Controlled. "You'll need to hop up the steps. Think you can manage?"

Ryan's jaw tightened, but he nodded. "I'll manage."

I hovered behind him as he braced himself against the railing and shifted his weight onto his good leg. Each small hop sent a flicker of pain across his face, but he swallowed it down. Stubborn.

"Take it slow," I muttered, my hand hovering near his back. "Last thing I need is you faceplanting in the doorway."

A dry huff of laughter escaped him as he steadied himself at the top step. "You'd never let me live that down, would you?"

I smirked. "Not a chance."

The cabin stood like a relic of another time—weathered, battered, but still holding on. The peeling paint and loose shutters rattled against the storm, their hollow clatter swallowed by the wind. The porch sagged slightly, but the roof held. That was enough.

Inside, the air was thick with dust and damp wood, the scent of long-forgotten fires clinging to the stone hearth that dominated one wall. Two worn chairs slumped near it, their fabric torn and stuffing exposed, like they'd given up long ago. A tilted shelf barely clung to the wall, its few remaining trinkets forgotten by time.

I maneuvered Ryan into one of the chairs, steadying him as the old wood groaned under his weight. He exhaled sharply, shifting in discomfort. "Cozy," he muttered, his tone as dry as the firewood I desperately hoped was salvageable.

A smirk tugged at my lips as I shrugged off my pack. "Hey, beats drowning, right?"

Ryan let out a low chuckle, some of the tension easing from his shoulders. The storm was still howling outside, rain hammering against the roof, but inside—inside, we were safe for now.

Dropping to my knees in front of the fireplace, I pulled out my waterproof kindling and fire starter, my hands moving on muscle memory alone. I'd done this too many times to count—in the rain, in the cold, in places far worse than this. Within seconds, a small flame flickered, hungrily licking at the dry wood. I coaxed the kindling gently, tending it until the fire caught and spread, pushing back against the chill in the air.

I turned to Chance, freeing my pack from his harness and placing it by the fire. "Time to rest those weary paws, you drowned rat," I said softly, scratching his ears. He answered with a satisfied grunt, gave one good shake to rid himself of raindrops, and then settled onto the blanket I'd laid out.

My eyes drifted to Ryan. He slumped in his chair, teeth clenched, shifting uncomfortably as his injured ankle protested each tiny movement. The rain had soaked him through, his clothes sticking to his frame and dark hair dripping steadily onto his shoulders. The dancing firelight only emphasized the weariness etched across his features.

I grabbed an emergency blanket, a bottle of water, and a protein bar from my pack, then crossed the room. "Here," I said, pressing them into his hands. "Eat something. I'll deal with your ankle in a minute."

Ryan accepted the items without protest, peeling open the wrapper as his gaze followed me. I could feel him watching—not with skepticism or impatience, but with something quieter. Something thoughtful.

I kept moving, scanning the space, mentally cataloging what we had and needed to get through the night.

No wasted motion. No hesitation. Control was every-thing—it was the only thing.

The storm raged outside, but I could manage this. I could fix this. One step at a time.

The weight of my utility belt hit the chair with a dull thud, my fingers already working the clasps of my rain-soaked jacket. I peeled it off, the cold air hitting my damp skin like a slap, but I barely noticed. Without hes-itation, I grabbed the hem of my shirt and tugged it over my head, tossing it aside. The black sports bra underneath was dry enough; that was all that mattered.

I moved with efficiency—every motion deliberate, prac-ticed. There was no point in shivering through wet clothes when we had shelter and fire.

Across the room, Ryan stilled.

I caught the flicker in his gaze, how his body went rigid—not in embarrassment or discomfort, but in some-thing heavier. I didn't have to follow his line of sight to know what he was staring at.

The scars.

I'd stopped thinking about them a long time ago. They weren't secrets, and I sure as hell didn't hide them. Raised, jagged lines across my shoulder, trailing down my arm—permanent reminders of battles fought and sur-vived.

I didn't acknowledge his staring; I just kept moving, unfastening my soaked cargo pants and stepping out of them. By the time I looked up again, Ryan's eyes had darted away, his jaw tight, his hands gripping the blanket I'd given him like he wasn't sure what to do with himself.

But when his gaze flicked back—when he actually *saw*—I felt the shift in the air.

His breath hitched. His fingers twitched against the fabric of his blanket.

The firelight danced across the metal of my prosthetic, casting a soft glow where my lower leg should have been.

His stunned silence stretched between us, thick enough to choke on.

"You—" His voice cracked. He swallowed hard and tried again. "You carried me... with *that*?"

I exhaled through my nose, shaking out my pants before draping them over the back of the chair. "Yeah, Anderson," I said evenly. "I carried you with *that*."

The disbelief was written all over his face like he was trying to piece together the last hour—how I'd climbed through the mud, hoisted him onto my back, and hauled his stubborn ass through the storm—all while wearing a prosthesis.

Like I hadn't done it before. Like I hadn't been doing it for years.

He opened his mouth, closed it, then scrubbed a hand over his jaw. He looked like he wanted to say something, but whatever it was, it got lost somewhere between his thoughts and his pride.

I sighed, grabbing a dry shirt and pants from my pack and pulling them on, the warmth of the fabric a welcome relief against my chilled skin. "It's a prosthesis, Ryan," I said, voice level. "Not a handicap."

I turned to him, arms crossed, meeting his lingering wide-eyed look with a raised brow. "*Now*, are you going to sit there gawking, or are you going to strip before you freeze to death?"

Faling for the Rescue is available on Amazon.

Hana York Books

Hearts on Duty Series

Sparks of Temptation

Love's Anchor

On Call for You

Investigating Desire

Falling for the Rescue

For a full list of titles, please visit Hana York's website

www.HanaYork.com

About the Author

♥

Hana York writes fast-paced, heart-pounding contemporary romance packed with irresistible heroes, strong heroines, laugh-out-loud banter, and just the right amount of spice to keep things sizzling. Her books are for readers who love grumpy men falling hard, fierce women who don't need saving, and the kind of chemistry that sparks off the page.

When she's not crafting stories full of love, tension, and toe-curling moments, you'll find her daydreaming about small-town charm, plotting ridiculous meet-cutes, and consuming an unhealthy amount of coffee. She believes in happily-ever-afters, overprotective heroes who don't stand a chance against their heroines, and that every great love story should come with a side of sass.

If you love forced proximity, off-limits attraction, sizzling tension, and romance that makes your heart race, welcome to the world of Hana York!

Follow Hana York for new releases, exclusive content, and behind-the-scenes fun! Visit www.HanaYork.com for more information.